# Princess Backwards

by Jane Gray

Illustrated by Liz Milkau

Second
Story
Press

Princess Fred lived with her parents, King Nancy and Queen David, in a castle not far from here.

Wait a minute, I hear you say. You have the names all wrong! Don't you mean *Prince* Fred?

No, that was not a mistake. You see, in this kingdom girls were given names like Fred or Morty, and boys were called Katherine or Emma.

Perhaps I should explain.

In the kingdom where Princess Fred lived, things were different from what you or I know.

When people woke up in the morning, they had dinner. Lunch was at noon, of course, and everyone ate breakfast when the sun went down.

When two people met on the street, they said,
"Morning good," or,
"You see to nice!"

Everything was the reverse of what you and I are used to. And everybody thought it was perfectly normal.

*E*veryone, that is, except Princess Fred.

The poor girl just couldn't seem to get the hang of things. She didn't like roast beef and Brussels sprouts in the morning. She often got her words muddled, saying, "How do you do?" when she meant "Do you do how?" And she was hopeless at walking back to front, watching where she had come from instead of where she was going.

Because of this, people nicknamed her "Princess Backwards." They whispered to each other that she would never learn to do things properly. When she pointed out that it's easier to walk if you can see what's ahead, they just sighed and told each other that she was a lovely girl — but so different!

Life in the kingdom was fairly peaceful, except for one small problem. Well, not all that small.

As I'm sure you can imagine, people do not sleep comfortably in their beds when there's a dragon around. And that's exactly what there was.

His name was Marvin, and although no one had ever seen him up close, everybody knew he was horrible. The shoemaker had heard that Marvin had once burned down a whole forest with one fiery sneeze. The baker said that, after burning the forest to a crisp, Marvin had gobbled up everyone and everything left behind.

Marvin was terrifying, all right. They all worried that one day he would come and try to eat *them*.

And sure enough, one day Marvin came.

Princess Backwards was out near the castle wall, practicing her walk. The problem was that, every few steps, she had to look over her shoulder to see where she was going, which gave her a real pain in the neck. If she stopped looking, though, she either bumped into someone, or tripped and fell down. She tried and she tried but she just couldn't seem to get it right.

Finally, after many bumps and falls, she threw herself onto a bench and cried, "I GIVE UP! I'll never be able to do it. I'll always be different!" Her eyes filled with tears.

Just then she heard strange stomping and snorting sounds, and smelled a faint whisper of smoke. She looked out over the castle wall. Can you guess what she saw?

You're right. It was Marvin, that horrible dragon! Princess Backwards knew at once who he was, for she had heard terrifying tales about him all her life.

"Guards!" she screamed. "It's Marvin! I mean — Marvin it's!"

The guards stopped in the middle of their game of scotchhop, and turned and stared. This was the first time the castle had ever been in danger, and they weren't sure what to do. But they snatched up their bows and arrows, and scrambled to the castle gates.

When the guards saw that it really was Marvin, they aimed their arrows and arched their bows. But they all had their backs to Marvin, and they were shooting blindly over their shoulders. The guards fired over and over again, but the arrows didn't even come close.

Princess Backwards gave a grunt of frustration, seeing that the guards couldn't possibly stop the dragon. She was certain that once Marvin reached the castle, he would burn down the drawbridge with one fiery breath, and they would all be gobbled up.

There was only one thing to do.

Princess Backwards ran through the castle gates, past the shrieking crowds (who had also realized that things weren't going well for the guards), pausing only long enough to scoop a large bucketful of water from the moat.

She raced across the drawbridge and sprinted as fast as she could toward the dragon. She was in such a hurry that she forgot to run back to front, and forgot about looking over her shoulder. Instead, she ran face forward, head on, straight up to the dragon's great, clawed, dragonly feet.

Just as she got close enough to look right into his nasty, dragonly eyes, she lifted up the bucket and — WHOOSH! — hurled the water into his flaming, dragonly mouth.

Well, I don't know who was more surprised, Princess Backwards or the dragon. Both stopped dead in their tracks and stared at one another. All the people on the castle wall fell silent. Queen David held her breath, and King Nancy hardly dared to open his eyes.

Then the dragon spoke.

"Thank you, thank you, THANK YOU!" he bellowed. "You can't imagine how my mouth has been burning all these years. I tried to drink from the river, but the water turned to steam before I could swallow. I tried to brush my teeth, but I scorched all the bristles on my toothbrush. And when I opened my mouth to ask for help, I burned up everything in sight. You've made me so happy! Thank you!" And he picked up the princess in a great, dragonly hug.

Princess Backwards didn't know what to say. Imagine that — they'd been so afraid of Marvin for so long, and all he had ever wanted was a big drink of water!

"You're welcome," she replied, smiling.

While all this was going on, the crowds on the wall were murmuring in amazement. Princess Backwards, who couldn't seem to do anything the proper way, had saved the castle!

Finally, a great cheer rose up.

"Princess the for hurray!" everyone cried. "Marvin for hurray! Hurray, Fred!"

From that day forward, Princess Fred and Marvin were good friends. She taught the guards how to shoot arrows frontward, and Marvin became the fire marshal for the kingdom. And no one thought there was anything wrong about Fred being a little different, because they realized that different wasn't wrong. It was just different.

And sometimes, different is a lovely thing to be.

*For Emma and Katie*
— J.G.

*For S.B.*
— L.M.

NATIONAL LIBRARY OF CANADA CATALOGUING IN PUBLICATION DATA

Gray, Jane, 1968-
Princess Backwards / by Jane Gray ; illustrated by Liz Milkau.

ISBN 1-896764-64-9

I. Milkau, Liz II. Title.

PS8563.R4095P75 2002    jC813'.6    C2002-903668-2    PZ7

Edited by Gena Gorrell
Designed by Laura McCurdy

Printed in Hong Kong, China

*Second Story Press gratefully acknowledges the assistance of the Ontario Arts Council and
the Canada Council for the Arts for our publishing program. We acknowledge the
financial support of the Government of Canada through the Book Publishing
Industry Development Program.*

ONTARIO ARTS COUNCIL
CONSEIL DES ARTS DE L'ONTARIO

Canada Council    Conseil des Arts
for the Arts      du Canada

Published by
SECOND STORY PRESS
720 Bathurst Street, Suite 301
Toronto, ON
M5S 2R4

www.secondstorypress.on.ca